W9-CQP-975

Orp
and the
Chop Suey
Burgers

Other Avon Camelot Books by
Suzy Kline

ORP

SUZY KLINE is the author of the popular *Herbie Jones* books. In addition to writing, she teaches elementary school in Torrington, Connecticut, where she lives with her husband, two daughters, and three cats. ORP AND THE CHOP SUEY BURGERS is her second book about Orville Rudemeyer Pygenski, Jr., the hero of ORP.

Orp
and the
Chop Suey Burgers

SUZY KLINE

AN AVON CAMELOT BOOK

Special appreciation to Rufus, who made the chop suey burger recipe up, and to Jennifer and Emily, who ate them once a week.

And, as always, to my editor, Anne O'Connell, for her dedication and support.

AVON BOOKS
A division of
The Hearst Corporation
1350 Avenue of the Americas
New York, New York 10019

First Avon Camelot Printing: April 1992

CAMELOT TRADEMARK REG. U.S. PAT. OFF. AND IN OTHER COUNTRIES, MARCA REGISTRADA, HECHO EN U.S.A.

Printed in the U.S.A.

OPM 10 9 8 7 6 5 4 3 2 1

For Martha Swihart Weaver,
my mother,
who laughs, listens, and makes
outings fun. I love you.

Contents

Orp
and the
Chop Suey
Burgers

One: It All Started At The Dentist's Office

"**O**RVIE!" MOM HOLLERED INTO THE bathroom. "You've been in there an hour now!"

Of course I was. I get my best ideas when I'm sitting in the tub. The window was halfway open so I could enjoy the cool breeze.

Today was September 21, the first day of fall, and I was listing all the exciting places in my atlas that I *didn't visit* this summer:

1. Cannonball, North Dakota
2. Deadman Mountain, Wyoming

3. Mudlake, Idaho
4. Porcupine Mountains, Michigan
5. Venus, Florida
6. Hanging Rock, Ohio
7. Poison Spider Creek, Wyoming

And then as my stomach started to growl, I found other neat places that I *didn't visit*.

8. Milk River, Canada
9. Bologna, Italy
10. Hamburg, Germany
11. Chicken, Alaska
12. Cheesequake, New Jersey
13. Turkey, Texas
14. Pudding River, Oregon
15. Sandwich Islands, Pacific
16. Altoona, Pennsylvania

"ORVIE! GET OUT OF THAT BATHTUB!" Mom yelled again.

I decided not to push my luck. I draped a towel around my waist and walked into the living room dripping a little water on the rug.

"Have you no morals?" my ten-year-old sister Chloe said, as she turned on the TV with the needle-nose pliers. (Our TV knob has been broken for six months.)

My sister Chloe had a pencil on her ear, as

usual. And, as usual, she was working on a book. "I thought you were writing the great American novel in your room," I said.

"I am. I'm just taking a break. Do you want to read what I have so far?"

I was mildly curious. "What's it called?"

"*Rhonda's Rendezvous in the Rain.*"

"Forget it." I knew it was another one of her romance novels.

"ORVIE!" Mom said, following me into the living room with a peanut butter sandwich and sour pickle on a plate. "I want you to take Chloe to the dentist for her six-month checkup and cleaning."

"MOM!" I objected. "This is Saturday—my day off! I've been slaving in seventh grade for nearly a month now. This is my day to RELAX!"

"Relax at the dentist's office," Mom ordered. "I have to clean house and do the grocery shopping. Your dad is busy."

It was a losing battle. Time to retreat. I knew how Robert E. Lee must have felt in the Civil War.

"All right," I grumbled, biting down on the sour pickle. "I'll walk Chloe to the dentist's office, wait for her, and walk her back home."

Chloe looked up from the television set. "Do you have to make lists for everything?"

"I'm good at it," I said. Then I stepped over my dog, Ralph. He doesn't travel to exciting places, either.

There's a definite smell in a dentist's office. I noticed it right away when I sat in a squeaky brown leather chair.

What was it?

Lysol? Toothpaste? Lavoris?

That was it.

It was the smell of Lavoris.

I got up and walked over to the receptionist, who was typing behind a glass partition.

"Yes?" the secretary said, opening the sliding door.

"Can you tell me how much longer Chloe Pygenski is going to be?"

"Let's see . . . she has a cleaning and checkup. And we'll need to do X-rays of her teeth. Probably another thirty minutes."

Thirty minutes seemed like a lifetime.

"We have some lovely magazines on the rack near the fish tank," the secretary suggested.

I guess she knew I was getting bored. "Thanks," I said.

I wasn't about to read a "lovely" magazine. Maybe I could count the number of goldfish in the tank.

I walked over to the forty-gallon tank and started counting. When I discovered the thirteenth fish, I noticed he was lodged underneath a ceramic bridge. It looked like an emergency situation so I rolled up my sleeve and plunged my hand into the water. It was cool. As my fingers touched the slippery belly of the goldfish, it surfaced to the top.

The poor fish was a goner.

I thought I'd better tell the receptionist.

"Yes?" She seemed surprised to see me so soon.

"Excuse me, but there's a dead body out here in the . . ."

"A*AAA*ugh!" the secretary screamed.

". . . fish tank." I finished.

The lady put her hand over her heart. I noticed her nail polish was the same color as the goldfish. "Oh, you mean a dead *fish*?"

I nodded.

"It's floating around the top now. Do you want me to give it a marine burial?"

"I'm not sure I know what you mean," she said.

Which meant she didn't know what I meant at all. "I can flush the dead fish down the toilet for you."

That was when she cringed.

"Just leave it. I'll tell Dr. Sodquist later."

I went back to the forty-gallon tank. "Sorry, pal. Looks like you're going to be floating around in there for a while longer."

I sat down and pulled out the letter that arrived in today's morning mail. It was from Jennifer Washburn. She came to visit in July with her parents all the way from Ohio. Her mother and my mother were high school pals. While she was here she helped me start an I Hate My Name Club. It was fun.

I began reading her letter:

Dear Orville,
　　Seventh grade isn't any better than sixth. There are two other Jennifers in my class. I told my teacher to call me Jenny Lee. Now there's no problem. There's a Jen, Jennifer, and Jenny Lee.
　　Want to call me that from now on?

Jenny Lee?

I thought about the name. Sara Lee made a fortune in frozen desserts.

Robert E. Lee was a great general in the Civil War.

There's even a line of jeans called Lee.

Jenny Lee?

I liked the name. It had a good track record.

My favorite class is science.
We're studying meteors and craters.
I didn't know comets were
called "dirty iceballs." I've been
watching for shooting stars. Tell
me if you see one.

Jenny Lee

As I looked at the red heart on the back of the envelope, I decided to start watching for shooting stars tonight. In the meantime, I put the letter back into my pocket and took out a pen.

All I needed was some paper to write on. I went back up to the receptionist and knocked on the glass.

She didn't act thrilled to see me again. "Excuse me," I said. "Could I borrow a piece of paper?"

She opened her drawer and took out a piece of stationery.

"Thank you very much," I said looking at the letterhead.

This could be fun, I thought.

I sat down and started writing to Jennifer. I mean, Jenny Lee.

Dear Jenny Lee,

Some people write on hotel stationery or picture postcards. Can you guess where I am?

You got it, Sherlock! The dentist's office.

I like your new name. It may make you rich and famous someday. I liked your letter and hope you keep writing.

Comets are awesome. I have a list of all the craters that were made by them. My favorite is Crater Lake in Oregon.

I can't believe the summer is over. I never went anywhere. Can you come back next June to visit again? We could watch for shooting stars and give them crazy names.

Well, I have to sign off. Chloe will be out of her checkup any minute. Be good to your teeth.

Orville

As I reread my letter, I looked at my name. Orville.

My full name is Orville Rudemeyer Pygenski. Junior. Most people can't even pronounce it right. That's why I use my initials and go by ORP. My family calls me Orvie or Orv.

Jenny Lee was the *only* one who called me Orville. It was one of the ways she made me feel special.

I folded up the letter and put it into my other pocket. Then I reached for a magazine that didn't look too lovely. (At least it didn't have a living room on the cover.)

As I was flipping through the pages, I stopped when I came to page 103. There was this big picture of Disney World.

Disney World.

I was probably the only eleven-and-a-half-year-old in Hartford, Connecticut, who had never been there. My best friend Derrick Jones went twice. Last summer he brought back giant dark glasses. For himself. He also brought me a souvenir. I was really impressed until I found out what it was.

A Mickey Mouse napkin slightly stained with french fries.

Derrick is too cheap to spend money on anyone. Except maybe Ellen Fairchild. He took her to the Wednesday matinee this summer when it was half-price admission. For Derrick, that's a major investment.

When I looked at the picture again I noticed there was an announcement underneath:

ENTER YOUR OWN ORIGINAL RECIPE USING FU CHOW SOY SAUCE AND WIN A TRIP FOR TWO TO DISNEY WORLD!
Just fill in the entry blank below.

Fu Chow. I remembered the name. It was on a bottle of soy sauce in our cupboard. At the end of the week that's about all there was in it.

Too bad I didn't cook. What an opportunity to travel!

The only things I attempted were semi-disasters. I made some burnt cupcakes during the summer and last week, when Mom had no mozzarella cheese, I chopped up a leftover pork-chop and sprinkled it over a frozen pizza.

I'm no chef.

Then I looked at the word, RECIPE, again. Hmmm, I asked myself—what *is* a recipe?

It's a list of ingredients and instructions.

I was good at making lists! All I had to do was make sure soy sauce was one of the ingredients. I could do some experimenting.

Why not?

What did I have to lose?

The dentist's office had something to lose—one page in their magazine. Sorry, I thought, but I needed the entry blank.

Just as I stuffed it into my pocket, Chloe appeared in front of me.

She looked so shocked, I thought she had walked into the boys' bathroom by mistake.

"I don't believe it," she said, sitting down in a daze.

"What?" I wondered if she saw me rip the page. I started to feel guilty.

"I have a cavity."

I tried not to smile too much. "Hey, it happens to the best of us."

"But I brush after *every* meal and sometimes in between!"

I sure knew about that. She was always barging in on me in the bathroom.

"So from now on I'm using this before and after meals."

I looked at what she had in her hand.

It was dental floss.

That was when I stood up. I didn't want Chloe stringing me along any further.

I had more important things to think about than cavity fighters.

Like, what can you do with soy sauce?

Two: The Chop Suey Burger Experiment

I STARTED OFF AT A DEFINITE DISADvantage. It was Saturday afternoon and there was hardly anything in the cupboard.

Mom was at the grocery store getting new supplies but I didn't feel like waiting.

I took a second look at the things that had probably been in our cupboard since World War II. The Fu Chow Soy Sauce was there, a can of creamy cheese soup, pickled beet slices, marinated artichoke hearts, and chop suey vegetables.

It was no bonanza.

The refrigerator was just as bad.

A piece of unwrapped bologna was curled up like a canoe. There was a cube of margarine with little pieces of broccoli mixed in.

Nothing I would want to use.

But when I pulled out the meat keeper, I discovered one pound of hamburger. Probably for tonight's dinner. Why not experiment with it and surprise the family?

I went back to the cupboard and started reading expiration dates. The most recent one was on the can of chop suey vegetables.

Fate.

That had to be the one!

I opened up the can and drained off the liquid. Then I poured the stuff into a bowl and mooshed it together with the hamburger.

It felt cool and slippery in my hands—which reminded me of that goldfish. I wondered if he was still floating around.

Back to the matter at hand. How many tablespoons of soy sauce? That was *strategic*. Two? Three?

Just then Chloe came barging into the kitchen. "What time is it?"

"4:00," and then when I said four, I decided to go with fate and measure four tablespoons of soy sauce.

"What are you doing?" Chloe asked.

"Making world famous hamburgers."

Chloe leaned over the bowl. "What are those long stringy white things in the meat?"

"Bean sprouts."

"They look like dental floss."

I held up my hands. There was meat mixture stuck to them. Slowly I wiggled my gooey fingers at my sister and spoke to her in my deepest voice, "THE FLOSS BURGERS ARE COMING . . . NOW . . . TO GET . . . *YOU*!"

Chloe screamed as I chased her around the kitchen. That was when Mom walked in carrying two grocery bags. As soon as she set them down on the table, she asked, "*What's* going on here?"

"Nothing," I said calmly, wiping my hands on my jeans. "How was shopping?"

Mom plopped down in a chair. "Tiring. The lines were so long. What are you up to?"

"I'm making dinner."

Chloe stuck her nose into our conversation. "It will be our last supper. We won't live any longer."

"Funny," I said. "So funny, I forgot to laugh."

"You two never stop, do you?" Mom said as she massaged her toes.

Then she looked over at the patties I was frying in the skillet. "What *are* you making?"

"Dental burgers," Chloe butted in. "You can floss *while* you eat."

"Speaking of the dentist," I said with an ear to ear grin, "did you tell Mom about your . . ."

"Ma! Orvie is being a pain!"

I grabbed a tea towel and snapped it at her rear end as she flew out of the kitchen.

"Hello, everyone!" Dad said as he entered the kitchen door. "Sounds like things are popping around here." He leaned over and smelled the patties on the stove. "What are those?"

"Don't ask," Mom said, wiggling her toes. "You'll find out soon enough."

Then she got up and walked out of the room. "Chloe . . . How *was* your dentist's appointment?"

Ahhhh . . . What joy! I thought.

At 5:30 P.M., the family was sitting down to dinner. I checked the oven timer, then remembered it didn't work. I thought it was about ten minutes.

I couldn't wait to hear the reviews of my chop suey burgers so I cut off a small piece and gave it to Ralph.

When he spat it out, I knew I was in trouble.

I decided to simmer the patties a few minutes longer.

"We're waiting for this dinner surprise!" Dad called from the dining room table.

"Coming!" I called.

I brought a big plate of seven and a half chop suey burgers into the dining room and set them down next to a bowl of salad Mom made.

"Smells good," Dad said.

Everyone took a patty. Even Chloe. She said she would try anything. She was starving.

Dad chewed the patty slowly.

Mom took a second bite.

Chloe kept poking at the white things in the meat with her fork.

"Well?" I asked.

"Deeeeeeelicious!" Dad said.

"Simply scrumptious," Mom said.

"You really think so?" I sat down and took a bite. "Wow! These are really good!"

"What do you call these delights?" Dad asked.

"Chop suey burgers," I said proudly. I was pleased I could come up with a name for them.

Chloe put her fork down. "Now that they're cooked they look like worm patties."

Mom glared at her.

"Chloe!" Dad scolded. "We are *still* eating."

Chloe pulled out a bean sprout. "You mean *some* of us are eating. I'm still picking."

"You are excused, young lady," Dad said. "You are being rude and sassy."

I tried not to smile.

After dinner, I went straight to my room and carefully typed up the ingredients and instructions on the entry blank. Then I filled in my full name and address.

FU CHOW SOY SAUCE

ENTRY BLANK

Name

Address

Name of Recipe

Ingredients

Directions

As I walked my chop suey burger recipe to the corner mailbox, I wondered . . . Could this be the beginning of my life as a world traveler?

Today Florida!

Tomorrow . . . around the world in eighty days!

I dropped the letter into the mailbox and flipped the lid twice.

Three: Sunday Outing

IF YOU ASK MY MOM, SHE'LL TELL YOU that our family goes lots of places.

On Sundays.

She calls them outings.

Sometimes we go to the plant nursery and she picks up another rose bush.

Or we'll go for a drive through Farmington and look at the expensive houses. "Look at the veranda!" she'll say, or "What a marvelous picture window!"

It's very boring.

The only thing that saves the day from being a complete disaster is that we usually stop for frozen yogurt. Chloe will order her usual—strawberry cheesecake with strawberry topping. And I'll have raspberry with the blackberry topping.

This Sunday we were having the outing in our backyard. Dad was barbecuing chicken, and Uncle Gus was coming over with his new girlfriend.

Mom said she hopes this is the one her brother might get engaged to. But, when I found out her name was Mary Smith, I doubted it. Gus Stasion marry Mary Smith?

Nah.

My uncle is kind of weird. He will have to marry someone with a complicated name like Pygenski. It's part of our family history.

I like Uncle Gus. He is my favorite relative. He works at a garage all day and fixes other people's cars. He never has time to fix his wreck, though.

I think it's funny when I call him up. He always says, "Hello, this is Gus Stasion's gas station."

He's a riot.

I saw his rusty truck with the sagging muffler

rounding the corner. I ran down the porch steps to meet them.

As soon as Uncle Gus got out of the truck he scratched his beard. "Hi, partner! Got the chicken on?"

"Yup."

"How does it fit?"

I cracked up. Then I noticed the girl wasn't laughing. She probably didn't get dumb jokes.

"Orp, this is Mary Smith. Mary, this is my nephew."

When she held out her hand, I looked at her nail polish. It was clear.

"Nice to meet you," I said.

"What grade are you in?" she asked with a smile.

That's what most people ask when they don't know what to say. "Seventh."

"How's school?"

"Okay."

I noticed she was tall. Most of Uncle Gus's girlfriends are.

"I can smell the chow!" Uncle Gus said walking around back.

Mary handed me a bowl of potato salad. "Can you take this to the table?"

"Sure!" I said, reaching for the red bowl. I

31

was hoping there were no pimentos in the salad. Mom always put those little killers in.

Chloe and Mom were playing canasta at the card table while Dad was hovering over the chicken. "Want to play partners, Mary and Gus?"

Mom knew not to ask me. I hate canasta.

Uncle Gus took two huge handfuls of tortilla chips from a big bowl on the table. Some people take vitamin C regularly. Gus? He needs a daily dose of tortilla chips to get through life. As he sat down to play, Mary sipped on some iced tea and sorted her cards.

The afternoon didn't turn out too bad. We played a little whiffle ball after the card game. I managed to hit a homer over the clothesline. Mary Smith kept score. She doesn't play sports.

During dinner I think my uncle grossed out Mary, though. When he was finishing his third piece of chicken, he cut up some small pieces and put them in his beard. "Want to have something to snack on later."

Dad and I cracked up.

Mom and Mary looked totally disgusted.

It was then that I decided for sure who I wanted to go with me to Disney World when I won the contest.

Uncle Gus.

Four: Mrs. Lewis's Resource Room

*E*VERY FRIDAY MORNING I GO TO THE Enrichment Resource Room. It's a neat place. You get to work on projects and study anything you want.

The resource room teacher, Mrs. Lewis, is *my* kind of person. She travels a lot.

Last summer she went to Nigeria to visit her relatives. The summer before that she went to Egypt. Usually she brings back souvenirs she can wear. Today she had two rings on each finger, four bracelets, and a long necklace with a sphinx on it.

When she talks she has an English accent. "I have news!" she said to the twenty of us sitting around long tables. "This year, our principal has asked our Enrichment Resource Room to think of booths for our 12th Annual Cornell Middle School Fair and . . . run them!"

We all cheered.

"It will be a splendid opportunity to use our organizational and leadership skills!"

"The resource room rules," Derrick said, as he clenched his fists and flexed his muscles.

I laughed. Derrick was no Arnold Schwarzenegger.

"Can we run the food booth?" Some eighth-graders asked. "It makes the most money each year."

Suddenly Derrick stopped posing like a he-man and began to drool. "Hmmm . . . money. Can I be treasurer and count the profits?"

I rolled my eyeballs. Derrick loved to count other people's money.

"Yes, Derrick," Mrs. Lewis said. Then she turned to the eighth-graders. "You can run the food booth, but let's be creative! Think of *other* things to sell besides the usual hot dogs, chips, and soda."

Ellen Fairchild raised her hand. I noticed she had her long brown hair pulled back with two wooden barrettes. Her face always looked like it was just scrubbed with soap. She smelled so clean.

"Yes, Ellen?"

"I work with my Uncle Herman on Saturdays at his pet shop so I could ask him to donate a kitten for a raffle."

"Splendid!"

I wondered if Mrs. Lewis knew how often she used that word.

"Do you need any help with your raffle booth, Ellen?" Derrick asked. "I can draw a neat cat."

Then he drew an eight with ears and a tail on a piece of paper and held it up.

We all cracked up.

Making the moves—that was Derrick's specialty.

Ellen smiled. "Thanks, but I'd like to work on this project by myself."

Derrick was wounded, I could tell. He slumped down in his chair and scribbled all over his cat drawing.

That was when I raised my hand. "I'm interested in world geography so I'd like to do a huge map and charge people fifty cents to throw darts at exciting places."

"SPLENDID! And it's *educational*."

Mrs. Lewis got off on that word, too.

Chloe stood up. "I'll assist my brother. I enjoy researching things. While he's sketching the world, I'll go look up exciting places in our atlas."

I covered my eyes. That was the one drawback about our resource room. It included students in grades five through eight. Chloe was a fifth-grader this year and an honor student, so she was in it.

"That's real cooperative learning," Mrs. Lewis said. "In fact, I'd like to encourage the other fifth-grader to join an older student in working on a booth."

The other fifth grader got up and joined the eighth-graders who were selling food.

Smart kid.

Chloe was already taking notes in the back of the room.

Actually I didn't mind too much that she was working on my booth. She was a hard worker, careful speller, and had neat handwriting. She could be helpful.

36

Ellen tapped me on the shoulder. "Do you think you could bring Ralph to our pet shop sometime?"

"Sure, why?"

"I'd like to take some pictures of my uncle shampooing a dog and display them at my booth. It might help people learn about good pet care."

"Ralph would love to be a star at your booth!"

Derrick stuck his head into our conversation. "Need any help cleaning the cages on Saturday?"

Ellen resnapped her wooden barrette. I decided it was knotty pine like our cupboard at home.

"We can always use help, Derrick," she replied.

Derrick beamed. Now he had reason to be hopeful. After she left, Derrick whispered, "One of these days I'm going to kiss Ellen Fairchild."

I looked around. Suddenly the conversation had turned deadly. If Chloe heard *one* word, I'd murder Derrick.

"It's true, you know."

"What's true?" I said, cutting a long sheet of mural paper.

"If we don't kiss a girl *before* eighth grade we'll be dweebs."

I stared at Derrick. Last year I would have walked away from this conversation, but this year things seemed different. I began wondering what it would be like to kiss Jenny Lee as I penciled in the continent of Africa.

"I see you agree with me," Derrick said, cracking up.

"What's so funny?" I asked. Then I looked down at the continent I had drawn. It was in the shape of two lips. Quickly, I erased everything and started over.

By the time I outlined Africa correctly and added Zanzibar, Derrick was still laughing. I decided to remind him he had a booth to do, too.

"I've got an idea for one already."

"What is it?"

"I could donate some birdseed and have people guess how much."

"Not bad," I said. "What would they win?"

"The birdseed."

Poor Derrick. I always liked the guy, but he had no sense of reward. Which reminded me, I had to come up with something. What if someone zapped three exciting places on my world map with a dart?

"Don't you need to plan your materials?" I asked Derrick.

"Hey, I'll bring in a card table and some fir tree branches to make things look woodsy. I'll set the salt shaker in the middle."

"Salt shaker?"

"That's what I'll put the birdseed in."

I shook my head. Ol' generous Derrick. He was donating a salt shaker full of birdseed.

"So, do you need some help?" Derrick asked.

He seemed to have everything organized. "Want to make the prizes?"

"Sure, what are they?"

I decided to think fast. Most people like certificates. "Make some blue ribbons on cards."

Derrick nodded and then walked over to the supply shelf, got a pack of index cards and a blue magic marker. "How many do you want?"

"Lots."

Chloe came over just when I was sketching Mongolia and Derrick was halfway through the pack.

"Well, Orv, I'm getting to be a list-maker like you!"

I looked up and wondered.

"I found twelve exciting places in the world for our map."

Derrick put his blue marker on his ear but forgot to put the cap on. A blue streak was smeared on the side of his head.

Chloe was too engrossed to notice.

"Let's hear 'em," Derrick said.

Chloe began reading:

1. Honey Harbour, Ontario
2. Romance, West Virginia
3. Marree, Australia
4. Starlight, Indiana
5. Love, Mississippi
6. Tickle Bay, Newfoundland
7. Moon Lake, California
8. Wedington, Arkansas
9. Dayton, Ohio
10. Heart's Desire, Newfoundland
11. Prome, Burma
12. Kissimmee, Florida

Derrick raised his eyebrows up and down. "I'd like to take you-know-who to one of those places. I'll be first in line to throw a dart!"

I jabbed Derrick, then glared at Chloe. "Forget it! Save that stuff for your romance novels. Find some more places like these. . . ," I grumbled, scribbling down some names I remembered from the list I made in the bathtub.

Chloe shrugged. "So I'll have twelve neat rendezvous for my novel."

I cringed.

An hour later—after I penciled in all seven continents and seven oceans, after Derrick finished the certificates, and after Ellen covered her cardboard display with yellow paper and the words, GOOD PET CARE—Chloe returned.

"I continued your list, Chef Orp."

"Huh?" Derrick said.

I didn't feel like explaining the cooking contest. I hadn't heard yet. "You mean like the one that had Milk River, Canada?" I said making sure she understood.

Chloe nodded.

"Okay," I said. "Let's hear it then."

Chloe took the pencil off her ear and began reciting:

1. Bread Loaf, Vermont
2. Orange, France
3. Jam, Iran
4. Onion Lake, Saskatchewan
5. Egg Lagoon, Tasmania
6. Bacon, Georgia
7. Soda, India
8. Banana River, Florida
9. Chile, South America

10. Chocolate Mts., California
11. Mayo, Peru
12. Lemon Grove, California
13. Pickle Lake, Ontario

I hooted and hollered, "All right, Chloe!"

Derrick was drooling. "Man, are those places for real?"

Chloe nodded. She likes to unearth interesting facts about things.

"Our map of tasty places in the world is going to be neat!" I said.

Chloe frowned. "Could we call it something else? Tasty places is a boring title for a booth."

"Okay, you're the writer," I said. She worked pretty hard on her research. She deserved to title it. "What did you have in mind?"

"Delectable Destinations," she beamed.

I tried not to cringe. It was a bit much. "Fine," I said. "But, you've got to spell it."

Five: Express Mail

*O*NE SATURDAY AFTERNOON IN OCTO-ber, I was sitting on the porch eating some peanut butter rolled up in a lettuce leaf and pretending I was smoking a Cuban cigar when the mail truck drove up.

That was strange, I thought.

Usually the mail came in the morning.

"Express Mail for Mr. Are-ville Road-mayor Piggin Skee," the mail carrier said.

I looked at the guy. Geez, I thought. Some people really butcher my name, but this joker did it the best!

"That's me," I said.

As I took the letter I wondered who would be sending me Express Mail and calling me Mr.?

Suddenly I looked in the upper left-hand corner of the envelope. It said FU CHOW SOY SAUCE CO.

"WOWEE!" I shouted tossing my lettuce cigar to the wind.

After I ripped open the envelope, I sat down and read it:

FU CHOW SOY SAUCE CO.

Dear Mr. Pygenski,

Your recipe for Chop Suey Burgers has been chosen as one of the thirty finalists for the New England Regionals of the Fu Chow Soy Sauce Contest to be held in Boston at the Excelsior Hotel November 1-2. Please let us know if you can participate in the cooking finals so we can reserve a complimentary room for you and a guest, and a space in one of the kitchens. An instruction booklet is enclosed.

We look forward to hearing from you.

Sincerely,

Won Song Foo

Mr. Won Song Foo
President
Fu Chow Soy Sauce Co.

"MOVE OVER WHOPPERS AND BIG MACS . . . CHOP SUEY BURGERS ARE TAKING OVER!" I shouted.

Then I ran into the house yelling, "EVERYONE GATHER ROUND RIGHT NOW!"

Dad jumped off the couch.

Mom came running in from the kitchen.

Chloe stormed out of her bedroom. She had a pencil and notepad in her hand. "What's going on here? A possible plot?"

"Do you see this Express letter?"

Everyone stared at it. "It's from the Fu Chow Soy Sauce Company!"

"Fu who?"

"Here, Dad, read it out loud."

Mom and Chloe listened to every word.

"Well!" Mom replied when Dad finished, "That's wonderful!"

"Let me shake your hand, son. This is bigtime!"

"You are going to be in a cooking contest in Boston?" Chloe asked slowly.

I nodded as I shook Dad's hand.

"*You* are a finalist?"

"Yup!"

Chloe started writing. "This *is* a possible plot. Can I go with him, Dad, so I can get the background for my next novel?"

"No way," I said. "I want to take Uncle Gus. Can I?"

"Sounds fine to me," Dad replied. "You'll need a chaperone. Go and call him now!"

I picked up the phone and dialed his garage.

After the eighteenth ring, he picked it up, "Hello, this is Gus Stasion's gas station."

"Uncle Gus, do you want to go to a cooking contest with me at the Hotel Excelsior in Boston November first and second?"

"Are you kidding me?"

"No! I'm a finalist in the Fu Chow Soy Sauce Contest."

"Free lodging?"

"Yup."

"Free eats?"

"Yup," I was getting excited.

"You got a chaperone, kid!"

"Thanks, Uncle Gus!"

Mom came running back into the room. "You can take my best apron for good luck."

I looked at the apron with the embroidered apples on each pocket. "No thanks, Mom. I'll use a tea towel and tuck it in my pants."

"So . . . you think you've got a shot at Disney World?" Dad said as he looked in the instruction booklet.

"I've always been a traveler at heart, Dad. This is my big opportunity."

"Well, why not!"

"My Orvie," Mom said. "My handsome son is going to Boston for the weekend."

"Please, Mom," I said. I hated it when she got that way. "I'll see you guys later. I have some letters to write."

When I got to my room, I bolted the door. Then I typed a short one to Mr. Won Song Foo and a long one to Jenny Lee. Now *two* people knew me as Orville.

Dear Mr. Won Song Foo,

    Thank you for your letter. I will be happy to participate in the New England Regionals in Boston, November 1-2.

                Sincerely,

                Orville Rudemeyer Pygenski

                Orville Rudemeyer Pygenski

Dear Jenny Lee,

    Remember when we made cupcakes?
    Well, you'll never guess.... I am
going to Boston November 1-2 to compete
in a cooking contest. My recipe, Chop
Suey Burgers, is one of thirty finalists.
Uncle Gus is coming with me.
    If I do win, and go to Disney World,
I'll bring you back a souvenir. What
would you like?
    I haven't seen a shooting star yet
but I'm watching every night out my
window. Maybe the same one I see sometime
over Connecticut will fly over Ohio.

                          Orville

P.S. I'm sending you the recipe. Maybe
you'll try it out.

P.S.S. I miss you.

When I reread my letter to Jenny Lee, I decided to white-out the P.S.S. It sounded too much like I was in love or something. I wasn't ready for that stuff yet.

Six: The Pet Shop

*A*S SOON AS RALPH AND I WALKED into Herman's Pet Shop, a voice squeaked, "Hello . . . hello!"

We both looked up. It was a big green myna bird chained to a tall wooden post.

"How are you?" it shrieked.

"I'm fine," I called out.

"Woof! Woof!" Ralph barked.

Derrick waved from a hamster cage. He was putting in some fresh wood chips. Ellen waved from behind the counter. She was tying a twisty to a bag of goldfish for a little girl and her father.

I wondered if the fish was related to my dead pal at the dentist's office who was still probably floating around.

"What's up?" Derrick asked.

"Great news! I'm going to Boston November first and second to enter a cooking contest and if I win I get to go to Disney World!"

"I've been to Disney World already," the little girl said as she walked out the door.

"I've been to Disney World twice," Derrick bragged.

"I've been to Disney World twice," the myna bird repeated.

Everyone laughed but me.

Derrick stood up. "You are going to be in a cooking contest?"

I nodded.

"Guys don't cook," he said.

Ellen slammed the cash register shut. "Excuse me, Derrick, but my brother *and* my dad cook at my house."

"Really?" Derrick tried to do some quick buttering up. "Hey, do you have any cookbooks I can borrow?"

I began to worry. This point had never come up before. How many guys were going to be at this cooking contest anyway? Was I going to be surrounded by girls?

Ellen continued her lecture. "Haven't you heard of the world famous chefs—Escoffier, James Beard, and . . ." she was running out of names as she was shaking her finger at Derrick.

". . . Chef Boy-Ar-Dee?" I added.

Uncle Herman laughed. "Well, congratulations, Orp! That's terrific. What's your prize recipe?"

"Chop suey burgers," I said proudly.

"Chop suey burgers?" Derrick cracked up. Then when he noticed he was the only one laughing, he stopped. "Can I pick those cookbooks up at your house today, Ellen?"

She half-smiled then she looked at me. "I'm happy for you, Orp. And thanks for bringing in Ralph. Uncle Herman, can you give him a shampoo now so I can take some pictures for my booth at the fair?"

Uncle Herman nodded as he started rinsing the sink.

Ellen took some fresh film out. "I got a new camera so I'm not sure how to put in the film."

"Need assistance?" Derrick sang out. "I know a lot about cameras. Sometimes loading them can be tricky."

"Thanks."

"We better go in the back room, Ellen, where it's dark though. We don't want to expose the film."

As I watched them go behind the curtain, I thought to myself, Was Derrick planning on getting his first kiss *right here* in the pet shop?

I looked over at the back room. It was cut off from the rest of the store by a long green curtain. The curtain didn't reach the floor. It was six inches short.

I could see Derrick's black sneakers and white socks. I also saw Ellen's sandals.

When the black sneakers moved closer to the sandals, I wondered. Is it happening?

When the sandals stood up on their toes, I *really* wondered.

"Everything's ready!" Uncle Herman called out. "Is the camera loaded?"

Suddenly the curtain opened and both Derrick and Ellen were staring at each other.

Derrick handed Ellen the camera. He looked like he was in a daze. "It's loaded with a . . . kiss now," he said. "I mean *film*."

They did it!

Ellen resnapped both barrettes and blushed. So, I thought, ol' Derrick finally got his *first* kiss.

I plunked Ralph into the sink. He was so big,

he barely fit. When he started licking my face, I thought to myself, one of these days I'll graduate from dog kisses.

Seven: The Good Luck Gift

*T*WO DAYS BEFORE THE CONTEST, I got a long brown package and a letter postmarked from Ohio.

I took the treasure to my room, bolted the door, and plopped down on the bed. Ralph hopped on the bed with me and watched.

"Just you can know about all this. My relationship with Jenny Lee is strictly personal."

"Woof! Woof!"

"I'm glad you understand, Ralph."

When I peeled away the brown wrapping

there was a long white box that was Scotch-taped on each side. After I removed the tape, I lifted the lid. Inside was a wooden spoon. Jen had written Orville with a curlicue in red permanent marker on the handle.

I started to laugh.

Then I hit Ralph on the rear end with it.

"My lucky spoon, see?" I said, holding it in front of my dog.

Ralph made a low growl and started pushing it away with his right front paw.

I loved the spoon. It was perfect. It was big enough to use as a spatula to flip the burgers.

I was so pleased with the wooden spoon, I almost forgot to read her letter.

But I didn't.

I opened it and settled back on my pillow. Ralph laid his chin on my chest and stared at the spoon while I read her letter:

Dear Orville,
How exciting to be in the cooking contest! I am sending you a good luck gift. I made the chop suey burgers. Dad had three!

I remembered her dad. Melvin! All he liked to do was eat and he ate everything—even my burnt cupcakes. If he liked my chop suey burgers, that wasn't such a compliment.

I loved them too.

I think your chop suey burgers are awesome.

Like you.

Jenny Lee ♡

I stared at the word "awesome" and the heart after her name.

"Well, Ralph," I whispered, "I think Jenny Lee has the hots for me."

Ralph made a high growl.

Then I jumped off my bed and said, "She thinks my chop suey burgers are awesome. She thinks *I'm* awesome!"

"Sounds like the makings of another romance novel," Chloe said through the door.

"Get out of here!" I shouted. Then I threw a shoe in her direction.

That night Ralph and I watched a lot of stars outside my window. None of them did any shooting.

No matter. I still felt terrific. I fell asleep that night holding my lucky spoon.

Eight: The Excelsior Hotel

MOM MUST HAVE REPEATED HERSELF three times, "Be sure to call us as soon as you get to the hotel room."

"Yes, Mom."

"And don't forget, I packed your red flannel pajamas. It's cold in November in Boston. I got Uncle Gus a pair just like them. They have FEET in them so you won't have to bring slippers."

Mom was acting like Boston was in another continent. Actually, it was just two hours and fifteen minutes away.

"And don't talk to any strangers, Orvie. You never know about some people."

Uncle Gus picked up my suitcase and then put his arm around his sister. "Orp is going to be twelve years old. He's a big boy now. Don't hover so much."

Mom kissed me on the forehead. "You're probably right. I just worry about things."

"Good luck, Orv," Dad said as he hugged me. "Remember to enjoy yourself. Winning isn't everything."

I bent down and gave Ralph a kiss on his black nose.

Chloe was standing by the door. She had a book in her hand. "Here, I went to the library and checked it out for you."

I looked at the title. It said, *How to Be a Winner in Three Easy Steps.*

"Thanks, Chloe," I said giving her a big hug. Sometimes my sister's research was helpful.

Then I took out my wooden spoon and waved it in the air. "I'm ready, Uncle Gus."

"Let's go, Chef Orp-Ar-Dee," he said placing a white chef's hat on my head.

"Where did you get this thing?" I asked.

"At Mr. Steak's Restaurant next door to the garage."

I laughed.

We climbed into his rusty truck with the hanging muffler and zoomed off.

Two hours later we stopped at the last toll booth on the Mass Turnpike. When I spotted the tall buildings and smelled the salt air from the Boston Harbor, Uncle Gus cracked one of his bad jokes.

"Why does the ocean roar?" he asked.

"I didn't know it did," I said.

Uncle Gus looked disappointed.

"Okay. Why does the ocean roar?"

"You'd roar, too, if you had crabs on your bottom."

"That's a knee-slapper," I said, rolling my eyes.

Uncle Gus didn't hear me. He was laughing too hard.

Fifteen minutes later we were in downtown Boston.

The Excelsior Hotel was huge. There were people everywhere! I didn't realize there were so many shops in a hotel. I saw a barber shop, a gift shop, a newspaper stand, and a beauty salon. There were places to buy candy and flowers.

One mother was walking around holding

onto two screaming kids. I was glad to be with my uncle.

He made me feel grown up.

The hotel room had two queen-size beds. We flopped down on them and felt like kings.

"Got a fifty-cent piece?" I asked when I saw the little sign, "Vibrator—50¢."

Uncle Gus plunked in a half dollar. Then he joined me on the bed. We jiggled up and down. "Aaaaaaaugh!" I said.

"Like it?" Uncle Gus asked, crossing his size thirteen feet.

"Love it! It's the fanciest place I've ever been to. The cleanest, too. What do we do now?"

"Well Orp, the actual contest is tomorrow morning. Most of the contestants are coming in tonight. We are supposed to meet everyone downstairs at 7:00 P.M. for dinner. I better call your mom and tell her we're settled in."

I didn't feel like talking to Mom so I hopped off the bed and walked into the bathroom.

I wanted to be on my own. I was beginning to feel like I was fifteen. Maybe sixteen.

When I got inside the bathroom, I noticed the sink. What a bonanza! I unwrapped the little squares of soap, unscrewed the caps on the little shampoo and conditioner bottles, and smelled everything.

There was a shower cap. I put it on and peeked around the corner.

"He's just fine," Uncle Gus said into the phone. When he looked up at me, he laughed. "Yeah, he's keeping warm."

I picked up Chloe's book and turned on the hot and cold water. I wanted to relax in the tub.

As I flipped through the book, I thought about the three easy steps to be a winner:

1. Dress like one.

What was I wearing? I'd have to go through the suitcase Mom packed for me, and pick out something with winning style.

2. Study your competition.

I figured I could do that at tonight's dinner.

3. Concentrate on doing your own thing.

No problem. Tomorrow I was not going to be distracted by anything.

After I got out of the tub and unpacked a few things, I asked Uncle Gus, "What kind of guys cook?"

"Oh . . . , the ones who like to eat, I guess."

"Really? But you eat and you don't cook."

Uncle Gus pulled the covers over his face and laughed. "You'll see them at dinner."

Nine: The Other Contestants

*A*T 6:40 P.M., WE WENT DOWNSTAIRS. The contestants were meeting in the Blue Ballroom. I hoped there wouldn't be any dancing. I didn't know how.

I danced once in the backyard with Jenny Lee, but that doesn't really count.

A woman with long black hair greeted us at the door. I noticed she had a name tag on. It said Trang Foo. I figured she was the president's daughter.

"Your name please?" She looked right at Uncle Gus when she said that.

I began to get worried.

"Orville Rudemeyer Pygenski, Jr.," I said.

"Could you spell that please?"

As I began to spell it, she ran her finger down a long list of names. There were about thirty of them. I noticed her long purple fingernail. It had little silver moons on it.

Uncle Gus noticed too.

"Here it is," she said and she started to put the name tag on Uncle Gus.

He put his hand on hers. "He's Orville Rudemeyer Pygenski, Jr. I'm his chaperone, Gus Stasion."

Trang Foo started to laugh. "Your name is gas station?"

"Gus Stasion. I know, it sounds like it, huh?"

She smiled. Her red lips reminded me of a candy apple. They were *that* red and shiny.

I think my uncle was noticing them, too.

Mary Smith was in big trouble!

"Oh, thank you for telling me," she said. And then she started to put the name tag on Uncle Gus again!

Now they both laughed.

I had a funny feeling I was witnessing love at first sight. Chloe missed a real scene here.

As Trang Foo put the name tag on my jacket, I thought of something.

Amazing!

If Trang Foo married my uncle, she would be Trang Stasion—that was weird!

Train station!

I shook my head and walked toward the Blue Ballroom. I began to wonder about how many kids would be in the contest.

When we stepped inside the ballroom, I found out.

"Oh geez," I said. "I am the *only* kid here!"

Uncle Gus patted me on the back and whispered, "Don't hang your head. You've done everything they have."

We sat down next to a potted plant. A waitress came over right away and brought us some tea.

A short man with a black mustache followed. His hair was cut into very even bangs.

"I am Won Song Foo, President of the Fu Chow Company. Welcome to the competition. I wish you good luck, young man."

He shook my hand and then Uncle Gus's.

I watched him as he went to the other tables shaking hands.

Most of the people there were women. Derrick was right. And most of the women looked like my mother.

Or grandmother.

"Do you think I look okay?" I asked Gus.

"Yeah, I like your blue pin-striped shirt. It's classy. Nice navy blue tie, too."

I straightened it a little. It was important to dress like a winner. That was Step One.

Just then Trang Foo walked up to the podium. I noticed Uncle Gus put his tea down and stared at her gold and black dress.

I stared at her black, lacy nylons.

When she got to the microphone, she began speaking. "I would like to welcome you all to the 10th Annual Fu Chow Soy Sauce Contest. Each of you is one of the thirty finalists chosen to compete for the grand prize of one week in Disney World."

One week! I thought. Man, I'd get out of school!

"We are also pleased to announce that there will be several other awards this year for second place, third place, and a special Honorable Mention."

The audience broke out into applause.

I looked around the room again. There were so many women I was beginning to get nervous.

"Are you sure I look all right?" I asked.

Gus didn't hear me. He was watching Trang Foo walk out the door. "Huh?"

"Do I look okay? Do I look fifteen or sixteen?" I didn't want to look like a kid.

"You're fine. Don't worry so much about how you look."

"Do you really think I have a chance to win?"

"I wouldn't be here if I didn't think so." Uncle Gus had a way of making me feel confident when I wasn't.

I looked over at the two gray-haired ladies sitting next to a marble statue. They were whispering. I wondered if they were whispering about me. Then another woman joined the two. She was about ten years younger and wore a blue suit with a checkered scarf. The yellow scarf reminded me of the flags they used in drag-strip races to tell the drivers they had crossed the finish line.

Of all the contestants sitting in the ballroom *she* dressed like a winner.

I noticed she was looking around. Studying the competition, maybe? Step Two. When our eyes met, it was like experiencing a laser beam. I think she thought *I* was probably going to be her toughest competition.

I knew she would be *mine*.

Ten: FIRE!

*U*NCLE GUS AND I TURNED IN AROUND 10:00 P.M. because we were tired, and I wanted to be fresh for the contest in the morning.

As we were snoring away around 10:45, this loud shrill alarm went off.

I opened one eye, "Is that our clock?"

Uncle Gus rolled over. "Reset it for another ten minutes."

I hit the snooze button and rolled over. The shrill alarm continued to blast.

Suddenly I sat up. Was it a fire alarm at the hotel?

Then someone banged on our door. "FIRE ALARM. YOU HAVE TO GET OUT OF YOUR ROOM IMMEDIATELY."

I threw back the covers and started shaking Uncle Gus. "Get up! There's a fire somewhere."

"Go away," Uncle Gus grumbled.

"IT'S FOR REAL! GET UP!"

Someone banged on the door again. "EVERY-ONE OUT!"

Uncle Gus threw back the covers. "No kidding, for real?"

"Yeah, let's go!"

Gus jumped out of bed. "Do you have any valuables you want to take with you?"

"Just my wooden spoon for tomorrow and my chef's hat," I said holding them up.

"I got mine," Uncle Gus said grabbing his bag of tortilla chips.

When we got out into the hall, we saw other people hurrying for the lobby.

I felt kind of dumb in my red winter pajamas, but there was no time to change. I didn't pack a bathrobe.

Uncle Gus didn't, either.

We must have looked like twins.

When we got to the lobby, Trang Foo was ushering people out the door. She still had her gold and black dress on.

Suddenly Gus saw himself in the lobby mirror. "Geez," he said looking down at his slippered feet, "do I look like a complete fool?"

He did.

But I wasn't going to tell *him* that. "Remember what you told me last night at dinner?"

"No."

"You said I shouldn't worry so much about how I look. Well, now I'm telling you the same thing."

Uncle Gus shook his head. "I'm going to kill your mother for giving us these Santa Claus outfits."

Uncle Gus stepped on the rubber mat and the hotel doors opened. About eighty people had gathered outside where the taxis were parked.

We stood next to a bush. When Uncle Gus saw Trang Foo, he stood behind it.

She had several elderly people on her arm. They must have been relatives. When she looked over at us, she started to laugh. "Are you two a dance team?" she called.

Uncle Gus didn't laugh. It was the first time I didn't see him laugh at a joke.

He opened up his bag of tortilla chips and started crunching loudly. A group of people who had party hats on and birthday horns looked over at Gus and whispered.

"I told you I looked like a fool," Gus mumbled with his mouth full.

Just then I saw a star shooting across the sky. It was awesome in the black, clear night. "Look! A shooting star!" I shouted.

Everyone looked up.

The streak of white light flashed across the sky like a bean sprout. My sign of chop suey burger victory tomorrow!

Fate.

It was meant to be all along.

Suddenly the fire trucks roared up the driveway. Eight fire fighters rushed into the building with their long black boots and wide black hats on.

Five minutes later, the Fire Captain appeared at the doorway smiling. "It's all right, ladies and gentlemen. Apparently a birthday cake had a lot of candles on it and set off the smoke detector."

Everyone laughed except Uncle Gus. He finished his bag of tortilla chips, then blew up the bag and popped it with his knuckles. It was not one of Uncle Gus's favorite evenings. I could tell.

I thought the night was exciting. Just before I turned off the light, I squeezed all the news on a picture postcard to Jenny Lee.

Eleven: The Contest

I REPORTED TO THE KITCHEN AREA AT 10:00 A.M. sharp. There were thirty different stations with numbers on them. I was number twenty-four. I was glad there was a four in it. Good old lucky four tablespoons of soy sauce.

The place reminded me of the home economics room at Cornell Middle School. Uncle Gus sat on one of the chairs near the door. There were about a hundred of them. You had to have a special yellow ticket to get in.

I noticed Trang Foo stopped by and said

something to him. He started to laugh. I was glad he got out of his grumpy mood.

The ingredients for my chop suey burgers were all laid out on the counter. The hamburger was in the little refrigerator that I shared with stations twenty-one, twenty-two, and twenty-three. I put my chef's hat on and placed my wooden Orville spoon on the counter next to the can of chop suey vegetables, the bottle of soy sauce, and some measuring spoons. A green skillet sat on the stove.

Mr. Won Song Foo went to the microphone. "Testing . . . one, two, three, testing . . ." Then he cleared his throat.

"Good morning, contestants. You will have one and a half hours to prepare your recipe. The judges will taste your dish as soon as it is prepared. Please ring the bell on the counter when you're ready for them."

I looked over on my counter. There was a metal bell there. It reminded me of the one at the butcher's. Mom always rang it when she wanted a pork roast sliced.

All the contestants were putting on their aprons. I did see a few men there. They had large barbecue aprons on. One of them, a short pudgy man about forty, had an apron with the words HOT STUFF printed on the front.

I took the tea towel off the kitchen rack and tucked it inside my jeans. No problem. I was ready now.

The lady at station twenty-two leaned over, "I think it's just wonderful that boys like to cook."

I smiled. I didn't feel like getting into any long conversation. I had important business to do. Concentration was Step Three on how to be a winner.

I noticed the woman with the checkered scarf was already stirring something over the stove. She was in station twenty-nine.

I opened the can of chop suey vegetables. As I drained them, a little of the liquid fell on the floor. No problem, I thought. If my mom were here she would have gotten out the big white mop and made a big deal about the importance of working neatly.

After I added the vegetables to the hamburger, I measured in four tablespoons of soy sauce. Then I mooshed everything together with my hands. That was always the best part—feeling the hamburger and slippery vegetables squish through your fingers.

The gray-haired lady in station twenty-two raised her eyebrows when she saw me massaging the meat. I waved to her with one of my gooey hands. She leaned back on her counter and grabbed a washcloth for her forehead.

I wondered if she thought it was wonderful that boys loved to cook now.

And what if she saw Uncle Gus's beard when he left food tidbits in it?

I enjoy being gross at times, too.

But now it was back to business. I rolled the hamburger into little balls and then clapped them into patties. I threw one hamburger patty into the air and caught it with one hand. Uncle Gus gave me the victory sign. I beamed.

James Beard would be proud of me.

I decided to flip one more hamburger patty into the air. Only this time I flipped it a bit much, it rolled over into station twenty-nine where the woman with the checkered scarf was working—my deadliest competition. I watched the hamburger patty with the bean sprouts roll onto the floor near her foot.

And then she stepped on it.

I was certain she would march over to me and tell me off. And I had it coming.

But she didn't.

She was too busy to notice the globule of hamburger guck which was now stuck to the heel of her black wedge shoe.

I shook my head. I felt bad about that. No

more flipping for sure. I took my lucky Orville cooking spoon and turned a few patties carefully in the green skillet. Then I lowered the flame and let them simmer. Ten minutes later, I rang the bell. Three judges came to my station.

I cut a juicy patty into six small pieces and then wiped my hands on the tea towel.

The judges took a fork and tasted one-sixth of the patty. It was such a small portion, I wondered how they would be able to taste the flavor. I also noticed the judges were accompanied by Trang Foo. She was carrying a clipboard.

"Hi, Orville," she said.

"Hi, Miss Foo." I smiled.

"This is Mr. Kackelman and Mr. Le Clare. We'll taste a few morsels of your recipe and then just jot down a few notes about our impressions. I'm sorry we won't be able to tell you anything right now."

I didn't really hear much of what she said. I kept staring at her fingernails. Today they were bright yellow with blue stripes.

Then I noticed her shoes. They were the kind with no toes. I could see her piggies through her lacy nylons.

I could also see the small puddle of chop suey vegetable liquid that I had spilled earlier. I was crossing my fingers she wouldn't get her toes wet.

"Oh!" Trang Foo said. "What did I step in?"

It was an emergency situation just like at the dentist's office with that dead goldfish. I ripped off my tea towel and dropped to the floor. After I wiped the liquid off, I dabbed her toes with a dry corner of the towel.

"I'm very sorry, Miss Foo," I said in a kneeling position. "I can be a real slob sometimes."

"Orville," she smiled. "Please get up. You don't have to be so chivalrous."

Chivalrous. I knew what that word meant. I read it once in a book about knights. Sir Orville? I liked it. I liked Trang Foo, too. Finally I stood up. "I really am sorry. I should have mopped it up twenty minutes ago."

"Well, we must move on. Thank you, Orville. You've been very thoughtful."

I watched Miss Foo, Mr. Kackelman, and Mr. Le Clare walk away. I wondered what they wrote down on their clipboards. Did they smile when they chewed a bite of my chop suey burgers? I couldn't see. I just remembered the yellow nail polish on Miss Foo's fingernails and . . . her toes.

Back in the hotel room, I told Uncle Gus everything. He laughed a lot. Then he noticed his digital watch said noon. "Well, we have one hour to kill before we go back down to the Blue Ballroom and find out the results. What do you want to do?"

I think he knew.

I was already running the bathtub water.

As soon as I got in, I yelled out a couple of questions.

"Did you mail my postcard?"

"Yup!" he called back.

"Did you read it?"

"Nope."

"Promise?"

"Nope."

"UNCLE GUS!" If he was getting nosy, I decided to do the same. "So what did Miss Trang Foo say to you that made you laugh this morning?"

"She said she . . ." and then when his voice trailed off, he poked his head around the bathroom door, ". . . she said she hoped she didn't hurt my feelings when she said we looked like a dance team last night in our red flannel pajamas."

"Oh? What did you say?"

Gus shrugged. "The truth. I said I was

crushed. Brutally wounded and that the only way I would accept her apology was if she let me take her out sometime."

I splashed some water his way. "What an operator you are!"

"Hey! She said yes."

I pushed the bathroom door shut. "Get out of here," I called.

Then I set my wooden spoon in the soap dish while I soaked in the tub. I needed all the luck I could get.

The results of the contest were in one hour!

Twelve: The Contest Results

*A*T 1:00 P.M., MR. WON SONG FOO STOOD at the podium with four envelopes. "We at the Fu Chow Soy Sauce Company would like to thank you all for your participation."

I moved around in my chair. It was hard to sit still. Then I popped a fortune cookie into my mouth.

"Did you take the fortune out first?" Uncle Gus whispered.

I pulled a long piece of paper out of my mouth. No, I didn't.

"What does it say?" Gus asked.

"I can't read it, it's too wet."

"Here, give it to me!" Uncle Gus squinted his eyes a little and then he held it up to the light from the chandeliers. "It says, 'YOU WILL SOON FIND OUT THAT YOU HAVE . . .'"

"Yeah?" I said finishing the rest of the cookie.

"You ate it, you big dummy!" Uncle Gus slapped me on the shoulder. "Pay attention."

"It was very difficult to choose the final three winners," Mr. Won Song Foo continued from the podium. "We shall begin by announcing the third prize . . ."

I liked the idea of starting with the last prize first.

"Third prize goes to . . . Mrs. Beatrice Lippman of Port Henry, New York, for her soy sauce apple pie!"

Everyone applauded. I couldn't imagine an apple pie with soy sauce in it.

Uncle Gus gave me the thumbs up sign. "Hang in there, Orp."

Mr. Won Song Foo continued. "Second prize goes to . . . Mrs. Alice Farmer from Brattleboro, Vermont, for her biscuit surprises!"

I couldn't believe it. It was the lady in the checkered scarf. Boy, could I pick the winners!

As she ran by our table, I noticed she still had hamburger stuck on the heel of her shoe. I shook my head and laughed.

The woman adjusted her yellow-checkered scarf and spoke briefly into the microphone. "I've never won a cooking contest before. I'm just thrilled. Thank you, Fu Chow Soy Sauce Company. Thank you. All of you." Then she threw a kiss into the air.

I thought the kiss was a bit much.

Mr. Won Song Foo lowered his voice "And now, ladies and gentlemen . . ."

I looked around and counted. There were just half a dozen gentlemen in the whole ballroom.

". . . the grand prize winner is . . ."

My heart started pounding. Could it possibly be me?

". . . the grand prize winner for a trip for two to Disney World is . . ."

The suspense was better than any Clue game Derrick and I had ever played, or any Monopoly game when we wondered if we were going to land on Boardwalk and have to pay $2,000 if there was a hotel there.

Nothing was like waiting to hear the name from the lips of Mr. Won Song Foo.

Mr. Won Song Foo ripped open the third envelope. "The winner is . . . Mrs. Rosie Ratterman from Bangor, Maine, for her soy sauce chocolate sauce!"

I fell back into my chair. A loser. What a disappointment.

Uncle Gus patted my hand. "Hey, you were a contender. You did a great job!"

But Mr. Won Song Foo continued talking. "You may notice that I have one more envelope here. It is a special Honorable Mention this year. It is an award for the tastiest recipe that is the easiest to prepare."

I looked at Uncle Gus.

Gus made the sign of victory using both hands.

"It goes to . . . Mr. Orville Rudemeyer Pygenski, Jr., from Hartford, Connecticut, for his chop suey burgers!"

I shot out of my chair like I was hit by a knob pulled back in a pinball machine.

As I raced to the podium, people stood and clapped. Even the lady with the checkered scarf was clapping.

It was kind of nice to have a fan like that.

"Your prize, Mr. Pygenski, is . . ."

My head was spinning with possibilities. A bike? I sure needed one. Mine was all rusted out. Or four passes to see the New York Yankees. While I was coming up with other ideas, I heard Mr. Won Song Foo say the prize.

And I couldn't believe it.

Five cases of Fu Chow chop suey vegetables.

"A year's supply!" Mr. Foo shouted with his hands in the air.

It was hard to smile. But I tried. I must have looked like a jack-o'-lantern. How can you get excited about canned vegetables?

"Thank you, Mr. Song Foo," I said. I don't think it was very convincing. As I walked down the steps of the podium, I kept my head down. I didn't want anybody to see how disappointed I was.

I had no idea what I was going to do with five cases of chop suey vegetables.

After Uncle Gus loaded them into the back of his truck, his muffler fell off.

We sounded like a garbage truck going down the Mass Turnpike.

Returning to Hartford with 120 cans of chop suey vegetables was a real bummer.

Thirteen: The Cornell Middle School Fair

*T*HE NEXT WEEK I WAS SOME KIND OF celebrity. It was hard to believe. The *Hartford Courant* ran a story on page eighteen about my cooking contest experience and took a picture of me sitting on my five cases of chop suey vegetables.

Dad kept asking me when I was moving them out of the garage so he could drive his car in.

What do you do with 120 cans of vegetables?

I asked Derrick and Ellen to come over and brainstorm ideas with me.

"Use them at the school fair this Friday," Ellen suggested as she sat down on a case.

"Yeah," Derrick agreed sitting next to her. "They could be prizes to go along with those certificates I made for your Throw a Dart at a Tasty Place booth."

"You mean Delectable Destinations," Chloe called down from the garage roof.

We all looked up. No one knew she was there. Sometimes Chloe says she needs new places to write. I guess she found one.

"You could write the winning recipe on those certificates," Chloe suggested.

"Good idea!" Ellen agreed, hopping off the box.

Derrick looked disappointed. He didn't even get a chance to put his arm around her.

"Your recipe won Honorable Mention!" Ellen exclaimed. "People will want to try your chop suey burgers."

Maybe, I thought. But I didn't feel like writing the recipe fifty times.

"We could divide the labor," Chloe suggested as she climbed down the side of the garage.

"Is the recipe long?" Derrick seemed worried. He doesn't like to work too hard.

"Nah, I know it by heart." Then I recited:

1 pound hamburger
1 can chop suey vegetables, drained
4 tablespoons soy sauce
Mix well
Shape into 8 patties
Brown and simmer for 10 minutes

"Dibs on writing 'Mix Well,'" Derrick said.

Ellen gave him a look. "That's not a fair division of labor. Right, Chloe?"

Chloe jumped to the driveway. "No, besides, someone has to write the name of the recipe and Orv didn't mention that."

I got the stack of blue ribbon index cards out of my room. I was glad I'd brought them home. I was thinking about writing WORLD TRAVELER on each one. At least people like me who don't go anywhere could still feel like a world traveler in a game at a booth.

We all lay down on the driveway and started an assembly line. Chloe started because she wanted to write "Chop Suey Burgers" in fancy cursive and then print "1 pound hamburger."

She passed the card to Ellen who wrote "1 can chop suey vegetables, drained." Derrick wrote "4 tablespoons soy sauce" (but he abbreviated T for tablespoon) and "Mix well."

Me?

I wrote "Shape into 8 patties" and "Brown and simmer for 10 minutes."

Derrick got the easiest job. He was always waiting for Ellen to pass him the card.

When we were halfway through, I got my radio and turned on some music. It was kind of fun being an assembly line for something I made up.

That Friday, the PTO hung a banner, 12TH ANNUAL CORNELL MIDDLE SCHOOL FAIR, across the courtyard.

At 3:30 P.M., an hour after school let out, the fair was in full swing. The booths were set up in the gym and our resource people were busy running them.

Mrs. Lewis was running around with a clipboard checking on this and that and saying, "Splendid!" Most of the PTO members were helping with the food booth, selling coffee and making change. The only new thing the eighth-graders came up with was pizza. They charged fifty cents a slice. It sure smelled good from where my booth was.

I looked over at Derrick. He was manning his Guess the Number of Birdseed and Win the Birdseed booth. No one was there guessing at his card table. The salt shaker full of birdseed probably wasn't too challenging.

The fir branches were a nice touch. At least Derrick's booth smelled woodsy.

Ellen was across the way selling lots of raffle chances for her little white kitten. It had a black spot on its neck. The pictures of Ralph in the tub turned out great.

Chloe and I were swamped with business. Everyone wanted to throw darts at our Delectable Destinations world map.

"I'll try for Hamburg, Germany; Mayo, Peru; and Pickle Lake, Ontario," a man said aiming his dart.

Zap!

Zip!

Whish . . . plunk!

He got them all but Pickle Lake. The third dart landed in the Arctic Ocean.

"Give me another three darts, son. I want to try again."

I handed him another set. When he finally got Pickle Lake, I handed him his copy of the chop suey burger recipe and a can of vegetables.

"Is this that recipe that was in the newspaper?"

I nodded.

"Great!" The guy went off smiling.

Ellen was right. People seemed to like the prize.

At 4:30 P.M., I couldn't believe it. Uncle Gus walked up to our booth.

With Trang Foo!

Chloe leaned forward, "Look at her nails! They are pink with purple moons on them."

"Shhh!" I said jabbing my sister.

"Hi, Orville," Miss Foo said. "Is this your girlfriend?"

I made a face.

Uncle Gus laughed. "This is my niece, Chloe."

Chloe put out her hand. I knew what she was doing. She wanted to see if those fingernails were for real.

"What are you doing here, Miss Foo?" I asked.

"Foo-ing around," she joked.

We all cracked up.

Geez, I thought. Trang was just like Uncle Gus and *his* dumb jokes. I think he met his match.

"Well," Uncle Gus said pulling at his beard, "I didn't get breakfast today so . . ."

He dropped two quarters into our coffee can and started aiming for the map.

He zapped three bull's-eyes: Egg Lagoon, Tasmania; Bacon, Georgia; and Milk River, Canada.

"Your prize, sir," Chloe said handing him the

recipe with the blue ribbon on it and a can of chop suey vegetables.

"What a good idea!" Trang Foo replied as she paid for three darts. "I didn't get breakfast either," she said to Uncle Gus.

I noticed my uncle was staring at her candy apple lips when she said that. I wondered if he had kissed them yet. Probably. My uncle was the fastest operator I knew.

Gus leaned over and whispered in my ear, "Want to bet she chooses the same things I did?"

I held up a can of chop suey vegetables.

"It's a deal."

Zip!

Zap!

Zing!

She hit three spots deadeye!

Lemon Grove, California; Banana River, Florida; and Orange, France.

Then she looked at Uncle Gus. "I prefer fruit. Your breakfast has too much cholesterol in it."

Gus frowned as he handed me his can of chop suey vegetables. He wasn't used to losing.

I hoped Mary Smith was.

She was history now.

Just after they left, I noticed Chloe was sitting

down on the gym floor writing madly in her notepad.

"Come on!" I complained. "I need your help. We have a line at our booth."

Chloe finished writing. "Yellow with red suns."

"Huh?"

"Rhonda's fingernails. Now she's ready for her rendezvous at Kissimmee, Florida."

Just as I was shaking my head, Mom stopped by. "Did you see Uncle Gus here?" she asked. "He said he was bringing a date."

"Yeah," I said. "They were just here."

"I knew it!" she said. "Do you think they're getting serious?"

I nodded.

Mom left with a big smile on her face. She really wants her brother to settle down. I think she's got the wrong partner in mind, though.

Fourteen: One Week Later

*T*HE CORNELL MIDDLE SCHOOL FAIR turned out to be pretty successful. According to Derrick, the self-appointed treasurer, we made $1,035.13.

That meant a lot of field trips!

We felt good about that.

But what *really* lifted my spirits was the letter the mailman brought on Saturday. It was postmarked Ohio.

Dear Orville,

    I got your postcard from
Boston. A hotel fire drill! A shooting
star! Wow! You had an awesome
time. I don't know- if you won or
not but if it doesn't interfere with
your travel plans to Disney World,
Mom said you could spend next
July here with us. Let me know.

          Jenny Lee

Spend a month in Ohio next July?

Where's my atlas?

I hopped into the tub and turned to the section on Ohio. What a bonanza! I started making a list of things we could do:

Place	Activity
Hanging Rock	Hang around!
Bass Island in Put-in-Bay	Fish
Bowling Green	Bowl
Rattlesnake Creek	Collect rattlesnake skins
Buckeye Lake	Swim
Coolville	Enjoy the breeze

When I studied my atlas more, I discovered some cities in Ohio that sounded like Europe:

Athens

Genoa

London

Malta

Rome

A world traveler at last!

A CAST OF CHARACTERS
TO DELIGHT THE HEARTS
OF READERS!

BUNNICULA   **51094-4/$2.95 U.S./$3.50 CAN.**
James and Deborah Howe, illustrated by Alan Daniel
The now-famous story of the vampire bunny, this ALA
Notable Book begins the light-hearted story of the small
rabbit the Monroe family find in a shoebox at a Dracula
film. He looks like any ordinary bunny to Harold the dog.
But Chester, a well-read and observant cat, is suspicious
of the newcomer, whose teeth strangely resemble
fangs...

HOWLIDAY INN   **69294-5/$3.50 U.S./$3.95 CAN.**
James Howe, illustrated by Lynn Munsinger
The continued "tail" of Chester the cat and Harold the dog
as they spend their summer vacation at the foreboding
Chateau Bow-Wow, a kennel run by a mad scientist!

THE CELERY STALKS   **69054-3/$2.95 U.S./$3.50 CAN.**
AT MIDNIGHT
James Howe, illustrated by Leslie Morrill
Bunnicula is back and on the loose in this third hilarious
novel featuring Chester the cat, Harold the dog, and the
famous vampire bunny.

NIGHTY-NIGHTMARE   **70490-0/$3.50 U.S./$3.95 CAN.**
James Howe, illustrated by Leslie Morrill
Join Chester the cat, Harold the dog, and Howie the other
family dog as they hear the tale of how Bunnicula was
born while they are on an overnight camping trip full of
surprises!

Buy these books at your local bookstore or use this coupon for ordering:
....

Mail to: Avon Books, Dept BP, Box 767, Rte 2, Dresden, TN 38225   **B**
Please send me the book(s) I have checked above.
☐ My check or money order—no cash or CODs please—for $_____ is enclosed
(please add $1.50 to cover postage and handling for each book ordered—Canadian
residents add 7% GST).
☐ Charge my VISA/MC Acct# _____ Exp Date _____
Phone No _____ Minimum credit card order is $6.00 (please add postage
and handling charge of $2.00 plus 50 cents per title after the first two books to a maximum
of six dollars—Canadian residents add 7% GST). For faster service, call 1-800-762-0779.
Residents of Tennessee, please call 1-800-633-1607. Prices and numbers are subject to
change without notice. Please allow six to eight weeks for delivery.

Name_____

Address _____

City _____ State/Zip _____

                                                   HOW   0391